Postman Pat® and the Secret Superhero

D0773995

SIMON AND SCHUSTER

"Da da DAA!" Charlie was zooming around the schoolyard in his superhero cape.

"The superhero in my comic book can fly!" he told Bill. "I wish I knew a real superhero."

"There's no such thing!" Bill chuckled.

"There might be!" said Charlie. "I bet there's one right here in Greendale – and I'm going to find him."

At the Post Office, Jess and Bonnie eyed each other up while Pat and Mrs Goggins sorted the mail! There was a big parcel for the Pottage twins, and a special delivery for Charlie.

"Righto, Pat," said Mrs Goggins, "I'm just off out to see Dr Gilbertson."

Charlie and Bill hid in the bushes. "Superheroes have to keep their special powers secret," Charlie explained. "We'll never find one if they think we're looking."

"What do we need to look out for?" asked Bill.

"Well, they're very brave and strong, and . . . WOW! Ajay's pushing that carriage with one hand! He's so strong, he must be a superhero!"

But a few seconds later, Ted appeared from the other side of the engine shed. He was pulling the carriage with the Greendale Rocket!

"So Ajay's not a superhero after all," giggled Bill.

Charlie sighed. "Let's keep looking. There's got to be a superhero in Greendale somewhere!"

As Pat set off on his rounds, disaster struck! He didn't notice that the back doors of the van had sprung open along the bumpy road . . .

. . . and by the time Pat and Jess arrived at Thompson Ground, there wasn't a single bit of post left in the van.

"Oh no," groaned Pat. "The letters and parcels have fallen out, Jess. We'll have to go back and find them."

Peering through the surgery window, Charlie thought he'd found his superhero!

First Dr Gilbertson disappeared behind a curtain, and Bonnie popped out, then Bonnie disappeared and Mrs Goggins popped out.

"Wow!" beamed Charlie, "Dr Gilbertson just turned into Bonnie – and Mrs Goggins!"

"Er, Charlie, I think all three of them were behind the curtain all along," said Bill.

"Oh," muttered Charlie sadly. "Well, I'm not giving up!"

Pat stopped off at Greendale Farm to check if Julia Pottage had seen any stray letters or parcels.

"No, I haven't, Pat, sorry," Julia told him.

Nobody noticed the parcel stuck up on the roof!

Katy and Tom were playing a ball game.

"Let's see if you can hit this," yelled Katy, throwing the ball at Tom.

Tom whacked it right up into the air. It headed straight for the roof, and hit a loose slate.

"Watch out!" called Pat. He caught the ball with one hand, and quick as a flash, moved Julia out of the way just as the slate came crashing down.

Then down came the parcel, and Pat leapt to catch it!
It was a new kite for Tom and Katy.
"Pat!" swooned Julia. "That was amazing!"

Charlie and Bill saw something amazing too! As they walked past the school, they saw Mr Pringle gliding across the room.

"He's flying!" gasped Bill.

"My dad's a superhero, and I never even knew!" squeaked Charlie.

Charlie and Bill burst into the room.

"Ah, hello boys, you can give me a hand putting these pictures up!" said Mr Pringle, sliding across the floor on his ladder.

"Oh no, not again!" moaned Charlie. "Dad can't fly. He's just got wheels on his ladder!"

Meanwhile, Pat was flying about all over the place, in search of the lost post! He balanced on a bridge to pick up a bright yellow envelope, climbed up a lamp-post to fetch a parcel...

...and leapt over garden fences to rescue some letters, before Rosie the goat ate them for her tea!

Finally, there was just one more parcel to find - Charlie's special delivery. It was right at the top of the hill, hidden under a hay bale. Pat gently took the parcel, but when he and Jess set off downhill, the hay bale came rolling after them!

"Uh-oh. Run, Jess, run!" Pat shouted.

Ted, Charlie and Bill watched in amazement as Pat and Jess raced towards the watermill, followed closely by a bale of hay!

"Look out, everyone," warned Pat. He tripped over a pile of rubbish in Ted's yard, and put his arm out to stop the hay bale - but Charlie's precious parcel shot out of his hand . . .

. . . and landed on the waterwheel.

Pat dashed inside the mill, ran up the steps, and leant out of the window. The parcel was just out of reach!

Pat jumped out of the window and onto the wheel. As he grabbed the parcel, the wheel began to move!

Pat ran faster and faster to keep up.

Then he somersaulted off, tumbled over the ground and jumped up onto his feet.

"Wow!" exclaimed Charlie, wide-eyed.

"That was brilliant!" admired Bill.

"Thanks," said Pat modestly, dusting himself down. "This parcel's for you, Charlie! Special delivery!"

"It certainly is," joked Ted.

"Thanks, Pat," smiled Charlie. "It's my new superhero comic book."

"You were right all along, Charlie," said Bill.

"Yeah!" agreed Charlie, "there is a superhero in Greendale - SUPERPAT!"

Pat grinned. "Hee hee, I'm no superhero, I'm just a plain old postman."

"Don't worry, Pat," whispered Bill and Charlie. "Your secret's safe with us!"

SIMON AND SCHUSTER
First published in 2007 in Great Britain by Simon & Schuster UK Ltd
Africa House, 64-78 Kingsway
London WC2B 6AH
A CBS Company

Postman Pat® © 2007 Woodland Animations, a division of Entertainment Rights PLC
Licensed by Entertainment Rights PLC
Original writer John Cunliffe
From the original television design by Ivor Wood
Royal Mail and Post Office imagery is used by kind permission of Royal Mail Group plc
All rights reserved

Text by Alison Ritchie © 2007 Simon & Schuster UK Ltd

All rights reserved including the right of reproduction in whole or in part in any form

A CIP catalogue record for this book is available from the British Library upon request

ISBN-10: 141693247X
ISBN-13: 9781416932475

Printed in the U.K.

1 3 5 7 9 10 8 6 4 2